WONDERING

IN LOVING MEMORY
OF MY FOREVER FRIEND
KATE POHL DOPIRAK
–M. F.

FOR ADAM
–R. J.

BEACH LANE BOOKS · An imprint of Simon & Schuster Children's Publishing Division · 1230 Avenue of the Americas, New York, New York 10020 · Text © 2022 by Meg Fleming · Illustration © 2022 by Richard Jones · Book design by Lauren Rille and Lissi Erwin © 2022 by Simon & Schuster, Inc. · All rights reserved, including the right of reproduction in whole or in part in any form. · BEACH LANE BOOKS and colophon are trademarks of Simon & Schuster, Inc · For information about special discounts for bulk purchases, please contact Simon & Schuster Special Sales at 1-866-506-1949 or business@simonandschuster.com. · The Simon & Schuster Speakers Bureau can bring authors to your live event. For more information or to book an event, contact the Simon & Schuster Speakers Bureau at 1-866-248-3049 or visit our website at www.simonspeakers.com. · The text for this book was set in Papercute, Harman Deco, Harman Elegant, and Harman Retro. · The illustrations for this book were rendered in acrylics on paper and then edited digitally. · Manufactured in China · 0122 SCP · First Edition · 10 9 8 7 6 5 4 3 2 1

Library of Congress Cataloging-in-Publication Data · Names: Fleming, Meg, author. | Jones, Richard, 1977– illustrator.
Title: Wondering around / Meg Fleming ; illustrated by Richard Jones.
Description: First edition. | New York : Beach Lane Books, [2022] | Audience: Ages 4-8. | Audience: Grades 2-3. | Summary: Illustrations and rhyming text show how wonder about little things in nature can lead to big discoveries.
Identifiers: LCCN 2021022433 (print) | LCCN 2021022434 (ebook) | ISBN 9781534449350 (hardcover) | ISBN 9781534449367 (ebook)
Subjects: CYAC: Curiosity–Fiction. | Nature–Fiction. | LCGFT: Picture books. | Stories in rhyme.
Classification: LCC PZ8.3.F639 Wo 2022 (print) | LCC PZ8.3.F639 (ebook) | DDC [E]–dc23
LC record available at https://lccn.loc.gov/2021022433
LC ebook record available at https://lccn.loc.gov/2021022434

AROUND

written by
MEG FLEMING

illustrated by
RICHARD JONES

BEACH LANE BOOKS

New York   London   Toronto   Sydney   New Delhi

WONDER
out the window.
A storm. A flash. A clap.

Trace the drops . . . a dot-to-dot
that makes a secret map.

Wonder down a pathway.
A nest. A bog. A trail.

Chik-chik chirp. Ribbit. Slurp.
Could that be someone's tail?

Wonder with a paddle.
A swoopy loop of jade.

Spinning swirl. Water curl.
Here comes the deep parade!

Wonder underwater.
Reflections trick the eye.

Floating on a spool of thought . . .
a fish might swim or fly.

Wonder underneath things.

It could be just a rock.

Then tiny feet become a street.
Look close. A city block!

Wonder down at footprints.

Who came?
Who left?
Who's here?!
To hide or play? I might not stay.

Oh wait. It's just a deer.

Wonder way up branches.
At all the wings that fly.

A leaf bouquet says
swip,
swip,
sway.

Hello, forever sky.

Wonder in the campfire.
A pop.
A streak.
A light.

A crackle spark twists through the dark,

repatterning the night.

Wonder out a pencil.

Or paint or stick or brush.

A thought. A shape. A great escape
that settles in a hush.

Think and blink on everything.
On wing. On foot. On fin.

WANDER

on the outside . . .

and **WONDER** on the in.